BIOGRAPHIES

SACAGAWEA

by Laura K. Murray

PEBBLE
a capstone imprint

Pebble Explore is published by Pebble, an imprint of Capstone.
1710 Roe Crest Drive
North Mankato, Minnesota 56003
www.capstonepub.com

Library of Congress Cataloging-in-Publication Data
Names: Murray, Laura K., 1989–, author.
Title: Sacagawea / by Laura K. Murray.
Description: [North Mankato, Minnesota] : [Pebble], [2021] | Series: Biographies | Includes bibliographical references and index. | Audience: Ages 6–8 | Summary: "How much do you know about Sacagawea? Find out the facts you need to know about this American Indian who helped guide the Lewis and Clark Expedition. You'll learn about the early life, challenges, and major accomplishments of this important American."—Provided by publisher. Identifiers: LCCN 2019055615 (print) | LCCN 2019055616 (ebook) | ISBN 9781977123336 (hardcover) | ISBN 9781977126580 (paperback) | ISBN 9781977123411 (adobe pdf) Subjects: LCSH: Sacagawea—Juvenile literature. | Shoshoni Indians—Biography—Juvenile literature. | Shoshoni women—Biography—Juvenile literature. Classification: LCC F592.7.S12 M87 2020 (print) | LCC F592.7.S12 (ebook) | DDC 978.004/9745740092—dc23
LC record available at https://lccn.loc.gov/2019055615
LC ebook record available at https://lccn.loc.gov/2019055616

Image Credits

Bridgeman Images: Wood Ronsaville Harlin, Inc., 21; Getty Images: GraphicaArtis, 23, MPI, 17, Universal Images Group/Encyclopaedia Britannica, 10; Granger: 14, 19; Michael Haynes: cover, 1, 13, 15; Newscom: Zuma Press/Kevin E. Schmidt, 5, 29; North Wind Picture Archives: 7, 9; Shutterstock: Alex Landa (geometric background), cover, back cover, 2, 29, Daniel D. Malone, 26, Everett Historical, 11, Michael Warwick, 27, Roark Nelson, 25

Editorial Credits

Editor: Erika L. Shores; Designer: Elyse White; Media Researcher: Svetlana Zhurkin; Production Specialist: Spencer Rosio

All internet sites appearing in back matter were available and accurate when this book was sent to press.

Printed in the United States
PO117

Table of Contents

Words in **bold** are in the glossary.

Who Was Sacagawea?

Sacagawea was an American Indian. She was a teenager when she met Meriwether Lewis and William Clark. She helped them explore the western United States. The trip was long and hard. She helped them speak and trade with American Indians.

People do not know everything about Sacagawea's life. But she was an important person in history. She was strong and smart. She helped make the country we know today.

Growing Up Sacagawea

Sacagawea was born in 1788 or 1789 near the Rocky Mountains. The area was not part of the United States yet. Today the area is the Lemhi River Valley in Idaho.

Her father was a chief of the Shoshone **tribe**. The Shoshone people moved often. They hunted **bison** and other animals. They gathered berries and plants. They lived in **tepees.** The tepees made it easy to move quickly.

American Indian tepees

When Sacagawea was 11 or 12, another tribe attacked. They were called the Hidatsa. They **enslaved** Sacagawea. They took her east. Today the area is in North Dakota. The Hidatsa lived with the Mandan tribe. They gave her the name Sacagawea. It means "bird woman."

These tribes did not move often like the Shoshone. They grew beans, corn, and other crops. They put Sacagawea to work. Then she was sold to a French-Canadian fur **trader**. He made her be his wife. His name was Toussaint Charbonneau.

a Mandan Indian village

Meeting Lewis and Clark

Soon Sacagawea's life changed again. In 1803, U.S. President Thomas Jefferson made a land deal with France. It was called the Louisiana Purchase. It included land west of the Mississippi River. The deal nearly doubled the size of the United States.

President Jefferson hired Meriwether Lewis and William Clark. He wanted them to learn about the land and the American Indians living there. Lewis and Clark needed many people to help on this long trip. Their group was called the **Corps** of Discovery. They left Illinois on May 14, 1804.

In October 1804, Lewis and Clark arrived near Sacagawea's village. They got ready to spend the winter there. They built a **fort**. It was a strong building with high walls.

Lewis and Clark looked for people to join their team. They needed people to show them the way through the land. They would need help speaking to American Indians along the way. In November 1804, Lewis and Clark met Sacagawea. She was 16 or 17 years old. She was soon going to have her first child.

Lewis and Clark meet Sacagawea.

Lewis and Clark knew Sacagawea could help them. She could speak with other American Indians. Lewis and Clark hired Sacagawea and her husband.

In February 1805, Sacagawea gave birth. Her son was named Jean Baptiste. People called him Pomp.

Two months later, the Corps of Discovery left to go west. There were more than 30 men. Sacagawea was the only woman. She carried her baby on her back.

Sacagawea was important to Lewis and Clark's group. She showed American Indians that their group was peaceful. A woman would not travel with a group that would attack others. She found berries and plants. The group used them for food and to treat sickness. She showed the men how to make clothes and **moccasins**.

In May, one of the group's boats nearly tipped. Sacagawea stayed calm. She saved important items like Lewis and Clark's notes. They named part of the river for her.

Sacagawea (standing in canoe on right) greets Chinook Indians.

Forgotten Hero

In August 1805, the group had made it to Sacagawea's childhood lands. She helped find the Shoshone. She was joyful to see her brother. He was the chief. The group traded for horses. Sacagawea asked an American Indian to help lead them over the mountains. They used canoes to go through the rough rivers.

Sacagawea on horseback as the group travels through mountains

In November 1805, the group made it to the Pacific Ocean. They stayed the winter. Then they made their way back home. They reached North Dakota in August 1806. The whole trip had lasted more than two years. Sacagawea's husband was paid. But Sacagawea was not paid anything for her work.

In 1809, Sacagawea and her family went to what is now Missouri. Clark wanted to send Jean Baptiste to school.

Around 1812, Sacagawea gave birth to a daughter. Her name was Lisette. Sacagawea soon became sick. Some people think she died December 20, 1812, at Fort Manuel. Today it is in South Dakota. Sacagawea was around 24 years old.

Sacagawea with her husband and son in Missouri

Clark took care of Sacagawea's children. Lisette may have died at an early age. Jean Baptiste lived to be 61 years old.

For many years, people did not know about Sacagawea's life. There were no pictures or drawings of her. In the early 1900s, people began to learn about her. They wrote stories about how she helped Lewis and Clark. Many women called Sacagawea a hero. They wanted people to remember what she did.

Some people said Sacagawea did not die in 1812. They said she lived to be very old. But no one knows for sure.

LEWIS ♥ CLARK EXPEDITION ♥ 1804
GEORGIANA HARBESON
1933
SACAJAWEA

Remembering Sacagawea

Today Sacagawea is an important person in America's past. There are schools, buildings, and places named for her. Sometimes her name is spelled different ways.

Places in the western United States are named for her. Lake Sakakawea is in North Dakota. Mountains are named for her in Wyoming, Oregon, and Idaho. People visit the Sacajawea Memorial Area between Montana and Idaho. It is near the Lewis and Clark National Historic Trail.

Sacagawea Peak in Oregon

People remember Sacagawea in other ways. There are many statues of her. A women's group made the first one in 1905. It is in Portland, Oregon. A U.S. dollar coin was made in 2000. It shows Sacagawea carrying her baby on her back.

Sacagawea was brave. She was taken from her home as a girl. She was treated unfairly. But she explored new places. She taught others. She traveled thousands of miles while caring for her son. Lewis and Clark could not have done their famous trip without her.

Important Dates

around 1789	Sacagawea is born in Lemhi River Valley, Idaho.
around 1801	Sacagawea is kidnapped by the Hidatsa. She is taken to North Dakota.
1803	U.S. President Thomas Jefferson makes the Louisiana Purchase land deal.
May 14, 1804	Lewis and Clark's Corps of Discovery begins its trip, leaving Camp Dubois in Illinois.
October 26, 1804	The Corps of Discovery reaches the Mandan and Hidatsa villages in North Dakota. Soon they hire Sacagawea and her husband.
February 11, 1805	Sacagawea gives birth to Jean Baptiste.
April 7, 1805	Sacagawea and the Corps of Discovery leave Fort Mandan.
November 1805	The Corps of Discovery reaches the Pacific Ocean.
August 1806	Sacagawea returns to North Dakota.
September 23, 1806	The rest of the Corps of Discovery returns to Missouri. It is the end of their trip.
around 1812	Sacagawea's daughter, Lisette, is born.
December 20, 1812	Sacagawea is believed to have died at Fort Manuel in South Dakota.

Fast Facts

Name:
Sacagawea

Role:
explorer

Life dates:
1788 or 1789 to likely December 20, 1812

Key accomplishments:
Sacagawea was an important part of Lewis and Clark's Corps of Discovery. She helped make contact and speak with American Indians along the way. She taught the Corps of Discovery to make food, medicine, and clothing from the land and its animals.

Glossary

bison (BYE-suhn)—a large, hairy wild animal that has a big head and short horns; sometimes called buffalo

corps (KOR)—a group of people acting together or doing the same thing

enslave (en-SLAYV)—to make someone lose their freedom

fort (FORT)—a place built to be strong to keep the people living there safe from attack

moccasin (MOK-uh-suhn)—a soft leather shoe or slipper without a heel

tepee (TEE-pee)—a tent shaped like a cone

trader (TRAY-dur)—a person who buys and sells goods

tribe (TRIBE)—a group of people who share the same language and way of life

Read More

Hadley, Emma E. *Sacagawea.* Ann Arbor, MI: Cherry Lake Publishing, 2019.

Lawrence, Blythe. *The Lewis and Clark Expedition.* Lake Elmo, MN: Focus Readers, 2019.

McAneney, Caitie. *The Life of Sacagawea.* New York: PowerKids Press, 2017.

Internet Sites

Sacagawea
www.ducksters.com/biography/explorers/sacagawea.php

Sacagawea: Montana Kids
montanakids.com/history_and_prehistory/lewis_and_clark/sacagawea.htm

Sacagawea: National Park Service
www.nps.gov/lecl/learn/historyculture/sacagawea.htm

Index